# Are You Sleeping?

Retold by MEGAN BORGERT-SPANIOL
Illustrated by ANNIE WILKINSON

CANTATA
LEARNING
MANKATO, MINNESOTA

**CANTATA LEARNING**

MANKATO, MINNESOTA

Published by Cantata Learning
1710 Roe Crest Drive
North Mankato, MN 56003
www.cantatalearning.com

Library of Congress Control Number: 2014938271
ISBN: 978-1-63290-073-9

*Are you Sleeping?* retold by Megan Borgert-Spaniol
Illustrated by Annie Wilkinson

Book design by Tim Palin Creative
Music produced by Wes Schuck
Audio recorded, mixed, and mastered at Two Fish Studios, Mankato, MN

Printed in the United States of America.

VISIT
WWW.CANTATALEARNING.COM/ACCESS-OUR-MUSIC

What wakes you up in the morning? The girl in this song can hear the ringing from a **bell tower,** a **grandfather clock**, and an **alarm clock**. She wants the rest of her family to wake up, too!

When you hear the morning bells, turn the page.

6

Are you sleeping, are you sleeping,
Brother John, Brother John?

Morning bells are ringing,
Morning bells are ringing,
Ding, dang, dong,
Ding, dang, dong.

Are you sleeping, are you sleeping,
Sister Jill, Sister Jill?

Morning bells are ringing,
Morning bells are ringing,
Ding, dang, dong,
Ding, dang, dong.

Are you sleeping, are you sleeping,
Father Jack, Father Jack?

14

Morning bells are ringing,
Morning bells are ringing,
Ding, dang, dong,
Ding, dang, dong.

Are you sleeping, are you sleeping,
Mother Jane, Mother Jane?

Morning bells are ringing,
Morning bells are ringing,
Ding, dang, dong,
Ding, dang, dong.

# GLOSSARY

**alarm clock**—a clock that a person sets to ring at a certain time

**bell tower**—a tower that holds bells; the bells ring to mark the time.

**grandfather clock**—a tall clock that stands on the floor

# Are You Sleeping?

Public Domain
Traditional

23

# TO LEARN MORE

Blair, Eric. *Sleeping Beauty: A Retelling of the Grimms' Fairy Tale*. Mankato, MN: Picture Window Books, 2011.

Gay, Marie-Louise. *Good Morning Sam*. Berkeley, CA: Douglas & McIntyre, 2003.

Pierce, Terry. *Sleepytime: Bedtime Nursery Rhymes*. Minneapolis: Picture Window Books, 2007.

Reasoner, Charles. *Twinkle, Twinkle Little Star*. North Mankato, MN.: Picture Window Books, 2013.

Schmidt, Hans-Christian. *Are You Sleeping, Little One?* New York: Abbeville Press, 2012.